A CRYPTIC CONFESSION

Down at my feet, a thin sheet of paper must have escaped the old leatherbound book of handwritten recipes I'd been examining. I retrieved it and laid it flat on the butcher-block table. It was written in Latin. Wes bent over it and started reading aloud. It was just like Wes to be fluent in a dead language.

". . . with grave suspicions that the purpose was to eliminate our most Reverend Father . . . Hey, Mad, this isn't a recipe. It seems to be . . ." He read on quickly to himself, and then looked up, startled. "It's signed by a Brother Ugo. And I believe he's confessing . . . to murder."

"Just when things were looking up," Wesley muttered. "Just when we were going to create the hippest party the pope has ever been thrown, you have to go finding a little old confession to murder."

"It's probably nothing," I said, tucking the page into a drawer. "It's so old anyway, it can't have anything to do with us."

"Oh baby," Wes said, smiling despite himself, "from your lips to God's ears."

Other Madeline Bean Catering Mysteries by
Jerrilyn Farmer
from Avon Twilight

SYMPATHY FOR THE DEVIL